ECHOES OF VELORIA

Echoes of Veloria

SATHYARAJ NATARAJAN

First Printing, 2025

"To the dreamers who refuse to give up,
To the wanderers who seek the unknown,
And to those who dare to break the loop—
May your echoes reach beyond time."

EPIGRAPH

"The past is but an echo, the future a whisper— only in the present do we shape our fate."

— Unknown

CONTENTS

PREFACE

The echoes of the past never truly fade.

They linger in the unseen, waiting to resurface, reshaping the present in ways we cannot foresee. When we first uncovered the anomaly, we believed it was a breakthrough-- an unprecedented window into time s hidden fabric. But we were wrong. What we had discovered was not just a loop in time but a doorway. And beyond that doorway lay something far greater, something far more dangerous than we had ever imagined. Now, as we step onto the alien world of Veloria, we are no longer just explorers. We are trespassers, caught in the currents of a story far older than humanity itself. With each step forward, the weight of the unknown presses upon us, whispering warnings in a language we do not yet understand. The past speaks. The future trembles. And in the present, choices will be made choices that will shape the fate of not just our team but perhaps the fate of entire worlds.

Welcome to Echoes of Veloria.

INTRODUCTION

Time is not a straight line. It twists, it folds, it loops. And sometimes, it echoes. What began as an experiment to understand the mysteries of time has led us here to Veloria, an alien world lost in the vastness of space, untouched and undiscovered by humanity until now. We came seeking answers, driven by science, by curiosity, by the unshakable desire to uncover the truth. But the truth, we are learning, is far more complex than we ever imagined. Veloria is not just a planet. It is a vault of forgotten history, a silent witness to forces beyond our comprehension. The very air hums with an ancient presence, and the shadows whisper secrets that refuse to be ignored. What we assumed would be a journey of discovery has become a fight for survival. The deeper we go, the more we realize that we are not alone here. And perhaps, we never were.This is not just our story. This is a story written across time, bound by choices and consequences. And as we step forward into the unknown, one thing is certainothing will ever be the same again.

PROLOGUE

The Lost Echoes

The stars pulsed like ancient beacons, their cold light stretching across the void to bathe Veloria in an eerie glow. Time had long abandoned this world, leaving behind only echoes-fragments of a past that refused to fade. A low hum vibrated through the planets desolate expanse. It came not from the wind, nor from the lifeless ruins that dotted the horizon. It came from beneath, deep within the veins of Veloria itself- a pulse, steady and unwavering, like the heartbeat of something waiting. Watching. In the depths of an obsidian structure, untouched for centuries, something flickered to life. Symbols etched into the walls pulsed with ghostly luminescence, their patterns shifting as if responding to an unseen presence. The silence cracked as a whisper-no, a message-rippled through the darkness. "They are coming."

A surge of energy rippled through the structure, racing through the forgotten corridors, igniting
machinery that had not stirred in eons. The air grew charged, dense with something neither living
nor dead.
And then just as suddenly as it had begun it stopped.
The whisper faded. The symbols dimmed. The pulse slowed.
The waiting continued.
Veloria had been silent for too long. But silence was never meant to last forever.

FOREWORD

Science fiction has always been more than just a genre it is a gateway to the unknown, a reflection of our deepest questions, and a canvas for the limitless possibilities of the universe. Echoes of Veloria continues the journey that began in **LOOPED**, taking us beyond the confines of Earth and into the heart of an alien world where the past and future collide. This book is not just a continuation it is an evolution. It delves deeper into the mysteries of time, consciousness, and the choices that shape destiny. Through the eyes of Dr. Aarav Menon and his team, we explore Veloria, a world that holds secrets far older than humanity itself. But with discovery comes danger, and the echoes of the past may hold warnings for the future. Writing this book has been a journey one filled with passion, curiosity, and an unshakable love for storytelling. I hope Echoes of Veloria captivates you, challenges your imagination, and keeps you on the edge of your seat until the very last page.

~ 1 ~

AFTERMATH

The lab was silent.

A silence so profound it felt unnatural, as though sound itself had been erased from existence. Moments ago, the chamber had been alive—pulsing with energy, vibrating with potential. Now, it lay still, dimly lit by the emergency backup systems. The air carried a metallic tang, thick with static and the unmistakable scent of burnt circuits.

Dr. Aarav Menon pulled himself off the floor, his ears still ringing. The last thing he remembered was the desperate attempt to shut down the experiment—the time loop growing out of control, warping reality itself. Then, the explosion of light. And now...

"Status report!" he barked, his voice hoarse but sharp.

A groan came from his left. Dr. Meera Raghavan was slumped against a console, blinking rapidly as she tried to focus. She clutched her arm, wincing in pain.

"I—I'm okay," she managed, her voice weak. "But the containment field... it's gone. The loop collapsed. We lost control."

Dr. Rajan Nair staggered to his feet, rubbing his temple. "That was more than just a collapse... That thing tore a hole through our calculations. Something else was in there, something we didn't account for."

Dr. Arjun coughed, waving a hand in front of his face as smoke curled up from one of the ruined consoles. "The energy readings... they spiked to impossible levels before we lost everything. That wasn't just a malfunction. That was an anomaly."

Aarav's mind raced. Anomaly. The word sent a chill through him. Their experiment had been designed to contain a controlled loop—a fraction of a second repeating endlessly within a confined space. But something else had happened.

Something—or someone—had intervened.

A sudden clang echoed from the far end of the chamber. The team snapped their heads toward the sound. The emergency lighting flickered, casting eerie shadows against the steel walls.

And then they saw him.

Sarren.

The alien figure stood amidst the wreckage of their experiment, his towering form illuminated by the flickering lights. His elongated features were unreadable, his eyes glowing faintly with an unnatural luminescence. His presence was both familiar and deeply unsettling.

Aarav felt his throat tighten. "Sarren..."

The alien tilted his head slightly, as though processing their words. Then, in his deep, resonant voice, he spoke.

"You have done something you do not understand."

Silence fell over the room again, but this time, it was heavy with dread. Meera swallowed hard. "What do you mean? The loop collapsed. It was unstable. We didn't—"

"No." Sarren's voice cut through the air like a blade. "It was never unstable. Not on its own. You made contact."

Aarav felt his pulse quicken. "Contact? With what?"

Sarren stepped forward, his movements fluid yet deliberate. "Veloria."

The word sent an immediate ripple of unease through the team. They had theorized about it—an unknown destination, a potential side effect of their loop experiment. But never had they imagined it was real.

Dr. Arjun's fingers twitched over the remnants of his console. "You mean... another location? Another world?"

Sarren's gaze was unreadable. "Veloria is not merely a place. It is a threshold. A gateway. And now, it has seen you."

Aarav's stomach twisted. "Seen us?"

Sarren let the words hang in the air before he spoke again. "They know."

A sudden tension gripped the room. Rajan exhaled sharply. "Who is 'they'?"

Sarren's expression darkened. "The ones who watch. The ones who do not wish to be found. And now, they know you exist."

Meera's breathing quickened. "Are they dangerous?"

Sarren turned his gaze to her, his glowing eyes locking onto hers. "They do not forgive."

A heavy silence settled over them, the weight of Sarren's words sinking in.

Aarav clenched his fists, trying to ground himself. "Then we have to go there. To Veloria. If we've made contact, we need to understand what we're dealing with."

Meera shot him a wide-eyed look. "Aarav, are you hearing yourself? We don't know what's out there. We don't even know how we connected to it!"

Sarren's gaze remained steady. "You do not have a choice. You have opened the door. Now you must step through."

The words hung in the air like an unspoken command. Aarav inhaled deeply, his mind already working through the possibilities. He turned to his team. "We need answers. We need to know what we've unleashed."

Dr. Arjun rubbed his temples. "And how exactly do you plan on getting to Veloria? The experiment is wrecked. The loop is gone. We don't even know if we can replicate it."

Sarren stepped forward, his towering presence filling the space between them. "I will take you."

Aarav felt a chill spread down his spine. There was no hesitation in Sarren's voice. No uncertainty.

Only inevitability.

The lab—once a place of controlled science—had become something else entirely. A gateway to the unknown had been opened, and there was no turning back.

Aarav took a deep breath and nodded. "Then we're going to Veloria."

Outside, the world remained oblivious to the events unfolding beneath its surface. But deep in the hidden corridors of ChronoX, humanity had just taken its first step into the abyss.

And something on the other side was watching.

~ 2 ~

THE SIGNAL

The remnants of the lab were bathed in an eerie glow from the flickering monitors, the scent of burnt electronics still heavy in the air. The damage was extensive, yet among the debris, something remained.

A pulse.

At first, it was barely perceptible, a rhythmic oscillation hiding beneath layers of static. But as Dr. Arjun sifted through the wreckage of their data logs, his fingers hesitated over the screen.

"Aarav... you need to see this."

The urgency in his tone cut through the haze of exhaustion. Aarav moved beside him, eyes narrowing as he scanned the display.

A waveform. Steady. Repeating. Alive.

"It's a signal," Arjun whispered. "And it's coming from Veloria."

The room fell into stunned silence. Aarav's breath caught in his throat. If the loop had collapsed, if their connection had been severed...

Then how was Veloria still reaching back?

The frequency pulsed again, like a heartbeat in the void. Meera leaned closer, her fingers trembling as she adjusted the filters. "It's not just a signal. It's... encoded. Almost like a message."

Rajan exhaled sharply. "A message? From whom?"

Sarren, who had remained still until now, finally spoke.

"Not from whom," he corrected. "From what."

Aarav met his gaze. "You mean... Veloria itself?"

Sarren's glowing eyes flickered. "Veloria is more than a destination. And now, it is calling you back."

The pulse quickened, as though whatever lay beyond the threshold had grown impatient.

Aarav clenched his fists. They had crossed a line.

And now, there was no turning back.

~ 3 ~

INTO THE UNKNOWN

The weight of Sarren's words settled like a leaden shroud over the team. Aarav exchanged glances with Meera, Rajan, and Arjun. Fear flickered in their eyes, but so did something else—an unspoken determination. They had come too far to turn away now.

Aarav took a deep breath, steadying himself. "If Veloria is calling us, then we need to be ready."

Sarren inclined his head. "You must understand—this is no simple journey. Veloria is a world unlike any you have known. It does not welcome travelers."

Meera crossed her arms. "Then why is it reaching out? If it doesn't want us there, why send a signal?"

Sarren's gaze darkened. "It is not an invitation. It is a warning."

The words sent a chill through the team, but Aarav refused to let fear cloud his judgment. He straightened his shoulders. "We need to prepare. If we're going to Veloria, we need every bit of data we can gather."

Arjun, still seated at the wrecked console, nodded. "I can try to stabilize the signal, maybe extract more details about what's on the other side."

Rajan ran a hand through his hair. "We don't even know how to get there. The loop collapsed."

Sarren turned to face him. "I can guide you."

Meera arched an eyebrow. "Just like that? You can just open a doorway?"

Sarren didn't blink. "No. But I can take you to someone who can."

Aarav frowned. "Someone?"

Sarren hesitated for the first time. "There are those who have traveled before. They do not belong to Earth. They do not belong to Veloria. But they know the path."

Silence fell over the group. Aarav's mind reeled with questions, but he forced himself to stay focused. "Where do we find them?"

Sarren's glowing eyes locked onto Aarav's. "We must leave immediately."

The team gathered what little equipment remained functional. The lab was a disaster zone, but Arjun managed to salvage a portable data module, and Meera secured the last working scanner. Rajan, ever the pragmatist, packed medical supplies and emergency rations.

Within the hour, they stood outside the ChronoX facility, the night sky stretching endlessly above them. The city lights flickered in the distance, oblivious to the monumental journey about to begin.

Sarren stepped forward. "We must move quickly."

"Where exactly are we going?" Aarav asked.

Sarren raised a hand, and for a moment, nothing happened. Then, the air before them shimmered, like ripples in a pond disturbed by an unseen force. Slowly, a shape began to form—a vessel unlike anything they had ever seen.

Sleek, dark, and humming with an energy that defied earthly physics, the craft hovered inches above the ground, its form shifting subtly as if adapting to their presence.

Meera inhaled sharply. "That's... not alien tech."

Sarren nodded. "No. It is older."

Aarav's pulse quickened. "How much older?"

Sarren's gaze was unreadable. "Before your history began."

Aarav swallowed hard. This was it. They were about to step beyond the boundaries of human understanding, beyond the safety of their world.

Arjun exhaled slowly. "No turning back now."

Rajan smirked, though his grip on his bag was tight. "Was there ever?"

Aarav took a final look at the world he knew, then turned to Sarren. "Let's go."

The ship's entrance slid open with a whisper, revealing the unknown beyond. One by one, they stepped inside.

As the door sealed behind them, the city of Earth faded from view. The stars stretched before them, and with a silent pulse of energy, the ship vanished into the void.

Veloria awaited.

~ 4 ~

THE JOURNEY BEGINS

The hum of the ship's engines filled the chamber as final checks were completed. The mission had shifted from theoretical discussions to cold reality. In just minutes, they would leave the safety of Earth behind and step into the unknown.

Aarav adjusted the controls, his fingers steady despite the weight of the moment. The coordinates were locked. The gateway, a shimmering ring of unstable energy, pulsed in front of them. It was a direct passage to Veloria—assuming the calculations were correct.

"Final check," Rajan called from the control panel. "Stabilizers, operational. Oxygen levels, green. Systems, all in sync."

Arjun tapped at his console. "No gravitational anomalies detected. We should be able to pass through without being torn apart."

"Should?" Meera raised an eyebrow.

"Well, this isn't exactly a commercial flight," Arjun said with a smirk, though his voice carried a hint of unease.

Sarren remained silent, standing near the viewport. His expression unreadable, his thoughts locked behind alien eyes.

Aarav exhaled, then pressed the intercom. "This is it. Everyone strap in."

The team settled into their positions, their seats locking into place. The countdown began.

Ten.

The ship's outer shell vibrated as the energy field of the gateway intensified.

Nine.

Aarav tightened his grip on the controls.

Eight.

Meera took a deep breath, her mind racing with the possibilities of what lay beyond.

Seven.

Rajan muttered a quiet prayer under his breath.

Six.

Arjun drummed his fingers nervously on the armrest.

Five.

The gateway's glow turned from a soft blue to an intense, blinding white.

Four.

Sarren finally spoke. "You must be ready."

Three.

Aarav's heartbeat pounded in his ears.

Two.

No turning back now.

One.

A sudden pull. A sharp jolt. The ship lurched forward, sucked into the vortex.

Then—nothing.

Silence.

For a moment, it felt like they had been swallowed by pure darkness. The sensation of falling, stretching, being torn apart.

Then—light.

The ship burst through the other side of the gateway, and the sight before them stole their breath away.

Veloria.

A planet unlike anything they had ever seen. A world with massive floating landmasses, glowing rivers of energy coursing through its surface like veins, and a sky swirling with colors beyond human comprehension.

Aarav barely registered the alarms blaring in the background. Their descent was unstable.

"We're coming in too fast!" Rajan shouted.

"I'm trying to stabilize!" Aarav gritted his teeth, pulling at the controls. The ship bucked violently, throwing them against their seats.

Sarren stepped forward, his voice eerily calm. "Brace yourselves."

The ship spiraled downward, straight toward the unknown world below.

~ 5 ~

DESCENT INTO VELORIA

The ship hurtled through Veloria's sky, its hull rattling under the force of entry. Blazing streaks of plasma flared against the windows as they plunged deeper into the alien atmosphere. Aarav fought with the controls, his hands steady but his pulse racing.

"We're coming in too fast!" Rajan's voice was tight with urgency.

"The thrusters aren't stabilizing," Meera shouted over the blaring alarms.

"Atmospheric density is higher than predicted," Arjun called out, scanning the fluctuating data. "If we don't slow down—"

The ship jolted violently as turbulence slammed into them, throwing Meera and Rajan against their harnesses. Sarren remained still, his eyes focused ahead, as if sensing something unseen.

Aarav gritted his teeth and pulled hard on the controls. "Engaging emergency thrusters!"

The ship trembled as the reverse thrusters fired, slowing their descent just enough to prevent an instant crash. But the landing was still uncontrolled.

"Brace for impact!"

The final descent was a blur of chaos. The ship streaked through the sky, diving toward a vast expanse of rocky terrain covered in mist. The ground loomed closer—

Then, with a thunderous crash, they hit the surface. The impact threw them forward, the ship skidding violently across the terrain before slamming to a stop against an outcrop of jagged black stone.

Silence.

For a long moment, no one moved. The only sound was the crackling of sparks from damaged consoles and the distant hum of the ship's failing systems.

Aarav groaned, forcing himself upright. "Status?"

Meera coughed, waving away a thin layer of smoke. "Still alive."

"Ship's in bad shape," Rajan muttered, checking his console. "Some systems are down. Power's fluctuating. But the hull held together."

Arjun unbuckled himself, wincing. "That was not the smooth landing I was hoping for."

Aarav turned to Sarren, who had barely moved. "You okay?"

Sarren exhaled slowly, his gaze shifting toward the window. "We have arrived."

Aarav followed his gaze—and his breath caught.

Beyond the fractured remains of their landing site, Veloria stretched out before them in breathtaking beauty and eerie mystery. Towering crystalline structures pulsed with an inner glow, casting a ghostly blue light across the landscape. Strange, luminescent flora spread in patches, their colors shifting as if reacting to their presence. Rivers of liquid energy coursed through the land, defying gravity as they twisted upward into the sky.

But it was what lay beyond that sent a shiver down Aarav's spine.

In the distance, partially obscured by swirling mist, stood a structure. A massive, ancient structure, rising from the land like a forgotten monument.

And it was not abandoned.

Faint, flickering lights moved within.

They were not alone.

~ 6 ~

SHADOWS OF VELORIA

The wind howled through the jagged terrain of Veloria, carrying with it an eerie resonance. The moment their boots touched the surface, a bone-deep chill settled over the team. It wasn't just the cold—it was something else. Something unseen.

Aarav tightened his grip on the small scanning device in his hand, its readings fluctuating wildly. "Atmosphere's thin but breathable," he murmured. "Radiation levels stable... but there's interference."

Meera exhaled sharply, her eyes darting to the swirling auroras above them. "What kind of interference?"

"The kind that shouldn't be here," Sarren said, his voice low. His tall form stood motionless, eyes locked on the horizon. "We are being observed."

A heavy silence fell between them.

Dr. Arjun, usually the most skeptical among them, shifted uncomfortably. "By whom?"

Sarren turned, his expression unreadable. "The ones who watch."

A sudden crack split the air, like ice fracturing beneath immense pressure. Meera spun around, her pulse spiking. "What was that?"

The ground beneath them trembled. Shadows flickered at the edges of their vision, moving in ways that defied logic. One moment, they were nothing more than shifting patches of darkness—the next, they were something else entirely.

"Life forms—" Rajan's voice was barely a whisper. "They're... blending with the terrain."

Aarav's breath hitched. The figures emerging from the darkness were unlike anything they had ever encountered. Their forms seemed fluid, shifting between humanoid and something far more alien. Their eyes—if they could be called that—gleamed with an unnatural luminescence.

Sarren tensed. "They do not appreciate trespassers."

Then, without warning—

A piercing shriek tore through the air.

The figures moved.

Fast.

Aarav barely had time to react before one of the shadowed entities lunged at them, its form distorting mid-stride. He stumbled backward, heart hammering. "Move!"

Meera pulled out a high-frequency pulse emitter and fired. The energy wave struck the nearest creature, and for a split second, its body flickered—revealing a skeletal, elongated frame beneath the shifting darkness. Then, as if adapting, it stabilized and kept coming.

"They're not affected by the pulse!" Meera yelled.

Sarren stepped forward, raising a hand. A strange, resonant hum filled the air, and the creatures halted. Their movements became erratic, unstable.

"They recognize me," Sarren said. "But they will not hold back for long."

Aarav swallowed hard, forcing himself to think. "Then we need to go. Now."

The team moved quickly, weaving through the jagged terrain, the creatures stalking them from the periphery. The deeper they went, the heavier the air became—charged, electric, alive.

Suddenly, a structure emerged from the haze.

Massive. Monolithic.

It loomed before them, its towering walls etched with pulsating symbols, radiating an energy unlike anything they had encountered.

Meera's voice was barely above a whisper. "Is that... a city?"

Sarren's expression darkened. "No. It is something far older."

A low, guttural sound rumbled from behind them.

The creatures were closing in.

And the only way forward was through the ancient, waiting structure.

~ 7 ~

THE FORGOTTEN GATE

The towering structure before them pulsed with an eerie, rhythmic energy, the symbols carved into its massive walls glowing faintly. It wasn't a city. It wasn't a ruin. It was something in between—a remnant of a past long forgotten.

Aarav could feel the weight of history pressing against his chest as they neared the entrance. The creatures behind them didn't attack, but they didn't retreat either. They lurked at the periphery, watching, waiting.

"What is this place?" Meera whispered, tracing her fingers over the pulsating symbols. The surface was cold, unnaturally smooth. It felt… alive.

Sarren's expression was unreadable. "The threshold."

Rajan frowned. "Threshold to what?"

Sarren didn't answer. Instead, he stepped forward and placed his palm against the wall. The ground beneath them trembled as the structure reacted to his touch. The symbols flared to life, intricate patterns expanding outward in a cascade of energy.

Aarav instinctively stepped back. "What the hell did you just do?"

The deep, guttural hum that followed sent vibrations through their bones. Then, slowly, the wall in front of them **split open**, revealing a passageway descending into darkness. A gust of air rushed past them—stale, ancient, filled with whispers too soft to understand.

Meera swallowed hard. "I don't like this."

"You should not," Sarren admitted. "But we have no choice."

Behind them, the creatures stirred. The flickering shadows moved in closer, their luminescent eyes narrowing. The moment the gateway had opened, their behavior had shifted. They no longer appeared predatory. They seemed... wary.

"They're afraid of this place," Arjun muttered.

Aarav exhaled sharply. "That doesn't exactly make me feel better."

Sarren turned to face them. "The path ahead is unknown, but the path behind is closing."

As if on cue, the terrain behind them shifted. The very ground they had walked on began warping, the creatures blending seamlessly with the twisting shadows. The air crackled with unseen energy.

Rajan's fingers tightened around his gear. "Then we move forward."

One by one, they stepped into the passage. The air inside was colder, heavier. The moment the last of them crossed the threshold, the massive stone doors **slammed shut** behind them.

Darkness swallowed them whole.

Aarav switched on his wrist light, the small beam slicing through the pitch black. The corridor stretched downward, its walls lined with more of the pulsating symbols.

"This place isn't abandoned," Meera murmured. "It's… waiting."

A shiver ran down Aarav's spine. "Waiting for what?"

The answer came in the form of a low, resonant **click**—a sound that echoed from deep within the structure.

Then, the walls began to move.

~ 8 ~

THE AWAKENING

The ancient structure loomed over them, its surface humming with an eerie, pulsating glow. Aarav hesitated at the entrance, feeling the charged air pressing against his skin like static. Behind them, the shadowy entities lurked in the darkness, their indistinct forms shifting restlessly. They hadn't pursued further—but they hadn't left either.

Sarren stood at the threshold, his gaze locked onto the intricate symbols etched into the towering walls. He reached out, pressing his palm against the cold, metallic surface. The reaction was immediate. The symbols flared to life, pulsing in a synchronized rhythm, and a deep, resonant sound vibrated through the structure.

Aarav exchanged a glance with Meera. "What did you just do?"

Sarren didn't answer. The doors—if they could be called that—groaned open, revealing a vast interior bathed in dim, shifting lights. The team stepped inside cautiously. As they did, the doors sealed behind them with a heavy thud.

"Great," Rajan muttered. "Now we're trapped."

"Not trapped," Sarren corrected. "Summoned."

The room they stood in stretched infinitely in every direction, its walls shifting and changing as if responding to their presence. The air crackled with energy. Strange symbols lined the floor beneath their feet, shifting under their weight, almost like they were walking on a living entity.

Meera activated her scanner, but the readings made no sense. "I can't get a solid reading. It's like this place is... distorting space."

Arjun crouched, running his fingers over the glowing lines on the floor. "This material—this technology—this isn't just alien. It's beyond anything we've ever theorized."

A low hum filled the space. The symbols on the walls rearranged themselves, forming what looked like an ancient language. A moment later, a voice—deep, layered, and unfathomably old—echoed around them.

"You have come."

Aarav stiffened. "Who said that?"

The light shifted. From the depths of the room, a figure began to materialize. Unlike Sarren, this being radiated a presence far more imposing. Its translucent form flickered between states of solidity and something less tangible. Tall, humanoid, yet distinctly otherworldly, its eyes burned with a piercing, silver light.

Sarren took a step forward and bowed his head slightly. "It has been long, Guardian."

A silence stretched between them before the entity finally spoke again.

"Veloria has waited. And now, the cycle begins anew."

Meera's pulse quickened. "What cycle?"

The Guardian turned its gaze to her. **"The cycle of truth and destruction. You have come seeking knowledge, but knowledge has a cost."**

Rajan exhaled sharply. "What does that mean?"

The walls trembled slightly, and the air grew heavier. The Guardian extended a hand, and the space around them began to shift. The walls flickered, transforming into moving images—visions of Veloria in its prime. Towering cities, civilizations thriving under alien skies. A harmony that spanned across time itself.

And then—chaos.

A dark rift split the sky. Beings unlike anything they had ever seen descended upon Veloria. War erupted. Cities crumbled. And then, the vision blurred into static.

Sarren's fists clenched. "The Fall..."

The Guardian nodded solemnly. **"Veloria was not always ruins. It was the pinnacle of knowledge, of unity. Until they came."**

Aarav narrowed his eyes. "Who?"

The Guardian's expression darkened. **"The Architects of the Abyss. And they are returning."**

A heavy silence filled the chamber. The weight of the words settled over the team like a crushing force.

Meera took a shaky breath. "And what does that mean for us?"

The Guardian's gaze bore into her. **"It means your world is next."**

The symbols on the walls pulsed violently. The entire structure seemed to tremble, as if something was stirring beneath its depths. A warning.

Aarav turned to Sarren. "Did you know about this?"

Sarren's jaw tightened, his eyes filled with something between regret and urgency. "I had my suspicions."

Meera's voice sharpened. "And you didn't tell us?"

Before Sarren could answer, the floor beneath them shifted. The chamber was collapsing, reality itself warping around them.

The Guardian's voice echoed one last time, urgent and unyielding.

"Decide, travelers. Will you run… or will you fight?"

And then—everything fractured into light.

~ 9 ~

THE UNRAVELING SILENCE

The air inside the monolithic structure was thick—oppressive, almost sentient. Every breath the team took felt weighted, as if the very walls were pressing in, whispering secrets too ancient to comprehend.

Aarav moved cautiously, his boots echoing against the smooth, obsidian-like floor. The luminescent symbols etched into the walls pulsed rhythmically, their glow neither warm nor cold but something in between—a presence rather than a light source.

"Does anyone else feel that?" Meera's voice was barely above a whisper.

Rajan exhaled sharply. "Feel what?"

She hesitated. How could she even explain it? It was like standing on the edge of a vast ocean, an abyss stretching before them—not physically, but in a way she couldn't define. It wasn't just the structure that felt alive—it was something beyond it, something waiting.

Sarren walked ahead, his gaze fixed forward, unreadable as always.

"This place remembers," he finally said. "It watches. It listens."

The words sent a shiver down Aarav's spine. He had learned to trust Sarren's instincts, even when they made little sense.

"Watches? By who?" Arjun asked, his voice unsteady.

Sarren didn't respond.

They pressed forward. The corridor stretched endlessly, its walls curving as if carved by something that understood dimensions beyond their own. With every step, the pulsing symbols grew stronger—reacting to them, acknowledging their presence.

Aarav's fingers twitched against his sidearm. He hated how vulnerable he felt here. He was a man of science, but Veloria was testing the limits of everything he believed in.

Then—

A voice.

Soft. Distant.

Yet it wasn't coming from their communicators. It was... everywhere.

"Turn back."

Aarav's pulse spiked. His eyes darted to the others. From their rigid stances, they had heard it too.

"Who's there?" Meera demanded, her fingers tightening around the pulse emitter.

Silence.

Then, the whisper returned, layered—like multiple voices speaking at once.

"You were not meant to arrive."

The lights on their suits flickered. Static crackled through their comms. The ground beneath them trembled, as if the structure itself was shifting, responding.

"Damn it," Rajan cursed, checking his scanner. "Electromagnetic interference is spiking."

Aarav tried to steady his breathing. "Sarren, what the hell is this?"

Sarren's expression darkened. For the first time since they had met, a flicker of uncertainty passed across his face.

"They know we are here."

Before Aarav could press him further, the corridor ahead twisted—no, **changed**. The walls shifted, bending in unnatural ways, warping as if reality itself was fluctuating.

A doorway appeared where there had been none before.

Not just any doorway.

A massive archway lined with symbols unlike anything they had encountered. Symbols that **moved**, rearranging themselves as if reacting to their presence.

Meera swallowed hard. "That wasn't there before."

Arjun took a hesitant step back. "We need to leave."

But Sarren... Sarren stepped forward.

"This is where the truth lies."

His voice was calm. Certain.

And then—

The door **opened**.

Beyond it, a vast chamber loomed. Not empty. Not abandoned.

And at the very center, something **waited**.

~ 10 ~

THE CHAMBER OF ECHOES

The chamber stretched before them, impossibly vast. The walls curved upwards, disappearing into a haze of shimmering darkness. It was as if the room itself refused to be fully seen, shifting between reality and something else—something unknowable.

At the center of it all stood a structure unlike anything they had encountered.

A **monument.**

Towering. Intricate. Carved from a metallic substance that reflected light in unnatural ways. It pulsed, not just with energy but with meaning—as if the metal itself was alive, whispering history through its shifting patterns.

Aarav's breath caught. "What is this place?"

Sarren stepped forward, his gaze locked onto the monument. "A record."

Meera shot him a sharp look. "A record of what?"

Sarren exhaled slowly. "Of those who came before. And of those who were lost."

A shiver ran through Aarav. "You mean... your kind?"

Sarren didn't answer immediately. His expression was unreadable, but something in his posture spoke of recognition—**and pain.**

"This is not just a monument," he finally said. "It is a warning."

A warning.

The words settled heavily between them.

Meera moved closer, running her fingers over the intricate carvings. The moment she made contact, a deep **hum** resonated through the air. The walls vibrated, the entire chamber responding like a living thing.

The carvings **moved.**

They **shifted**—forming images. Stories. Memories.

Scenes flickered before their eyes like echoes of a long-forgotten past.

They saw **Veloria before the fall**—a thriving world, its sky painted in iridescent colors, its cities standing tall, filled with impossible structures. They saw towering beings, not unlike Sarren, their presence commanding yet strangely serene.

Then—**the fracture.**

A darkness creeping in. Shadows seeping into the edges of reality, twisting the land, consuming the cities.

And then... **war.**

Explosions. Chaos. Figures fighting—some familiar, some monstrous, their forms blurred by whatever had corrupted them.

The final image froze Aarav in place.

A figure. **One of Sarren's kind.**

Standing alone amidst the ruins.

Facing an unseen force.

Making a choice.

And then—nothing.

The carvings went still.

The chamber fell into silence.

Aarav turned to Sarren, his voice barely above a whisper. "What happened here?"

Sarren's hands curled into fists. "Veloria was not abandoned," he murmured. "It was **sacrificed.**"

Meera's pulse spiked. "By who?"

A long pause.

Then—

"The Oathkeepers."

The air seemed to **freeze** around them.

"The Fractured Oath…" Aarav muttered, the words barely forming on his lips.

A new realization settled over them. This wasn't just a lost civilization.

This was the **aftermath of a betrayal.**

And they had just uncovered something that should have remained buried.

Aarav turned back to the monument, his heart pounding.

"We need to leave," Rajan said, his voice laced with urgency. "Now."

But the moment he spoke, the entire chamber **shock.**

The walls trembled. The monument's glow intensified.

And then—**the door behind them vanished.**

They weren't alone anymore.

Something **had awakened.**

And it had been waiting for them.

~ 11 ~

THE AWAKENING

The chamber trembled.

The intricate carvings on the monument flickered, their glow pulsating faster, as if responding to an unseen force. The air thickened, humming with an energy Aarav could feel pressing against his skin.

And then—**a sound**.

Not a voice. Not a scream.

A **resonance.**

Deep, guttural, vibrating through the core of their beings. It wasn't just sound—it was **words**, spoken in a language that bypassed the ear and sank directly into their minds.

"You have come too far."

Aarav's breath hitched. His vision blurred for a moment as something foreign brushed against his consciousness—an overwhelming **presence**, vast and incomprehensible.

The glow around the monument expanded, warping the chamber's dimensions. For a moment, it felt like they were **somewhere else**—a place that existed outside of time, outside of reality.

Meera grabbed Aarav's arm, her grip tight. "Tell me you heard that."

"I—" Aarav swallowed hard. "Yeah. Loud and clear."

Sarren, however, stood deathly still, his gaze locked onto the pulsing monument. His expression was unreadable, but his stance—**rigid, prepared**—told them everything.

He knew this was coming.

He had been expecting it.

A sharp hiss split through the air.

The carvings began to shift again, but this time, they weren't forming memories. They were forming **a face.**

Elongated. Alien. **Like Sarren.**

And then it spoke.

"Veloria does not forgive."

A violent pulse shot through the room. The force of it sent Aarav and the others staggering back. The very ground beneath them rippled, distorting as if reality itself was **fracturing.**

Meera struggled to stay on her feet. "Sarren—what the hell is happening?!"

Sarren's gaze was locked onto the glowing face. His fists clenched, and for the first time since they had met him, **he looked afraid.**

Then the voice spoke again, this time directly into Sarren's mind.

"You broke the Oath."

"You betrayed us."

Aarav barely had time to process those words before the walls of the chamber **split open**, revealing something beyond comprehension.

A **void.**

Endless.

Inside it, **figures moved**—tall, imposing, their forms flickering between solid and ethereal.

A council. A court. A **judgment.**

Aarav's heart pounded. "Sarren—what is this? Who are they?"

Sarren exhaled, the weight of centuries pressing against his voice.

"The Oathkeepers."

The figures **stepped forward.**

And Veloria itself **began to awaken.**

~ 12 ~

THE OATHKEEPERS' LEGACY

The weight of Veloria pressed down on them like an ancient force awakening from its slumber. Inside the massive structure, the air crackled with an unseen energy—almost sentient. The walls pulsed with shifting patterns, revealing fragments of history long buried. Aarav, Meera, Rajan, and Arjun stood motionless, their breaths shallow. At the center of the chamber, Sarren knelt before a towering monolith, his fingers grazing its surface as it responded to his presence.

"This is it," Sarren murmured. "The heart of Veloria. The last remnant of the Oathkeepers."

Aarav stepped forward, trying to make sense of the strange inscriptions. "The Oathkeepers... who were they?"

Sarren's expression darkened. "They were the protectors of knowledge. The last line of defense against forces beyond comprehension. They took an oath to shield Veloria's power from those who would exploit it. But their oath... was broken."

A sudden tremor rippled through the ground. The shadows that had been lurking in the periphery took form—figures cloaked in shifting darkness, their eyes glowing with an ethereal light. They did not attack. They watched.

Then a voice, deep and resonant, filled the chamber. **"The Oath was never yours to break, Sarren."**

A figure emerged from the darkness, its body flickering between solid and spectral. Unlike the others, it bore markings across its form, symbols eerily similar to those on the walls.

Meera gripped Aarav's arm. "Who... what is that?"

Sarren exhaled. "An Oathkeeper. One who survived."

The being took a step forward, its gaze piercing. **"You were meant to protect Veloria, Sarren. Not lead them here."**

Rajan raised a trembling hand. "Lead who? Us?"

The Oathkeeper ignored him, its focus locked on Sarren. **"You swore to keep the gateway sealed. And now it pulses with life once more."**

The monolith behind Sarren began to glow, its surface splitting apart, revealing something within. A swirling mass of energy—ancient, raw, and dangerously unstable.

Sarren turned sharply, realization dawning on his face. "No... this wasn't supposed to happen. The gateway—it's opening."

The Oathkeeper's voice deepened. **"And they are coming."**

A pulse of light shot from the monolith, illuminating the chamber in a blinding glow. Meera shielded her eyes. Aarav reached for Sarren, but the alien remained still, his face a mask of understanding and regret.

"We have to stop it!" Arjun yelled. "Whatever is coming, we—"

A deafening roar erupted through the chamber.

The figures in the darkness convulsed, their forms distorting violently before vanishing into nothingness. The walls trembled as the symbols across them began to crack apart, shattering like fragile glass.

Aarav grabbed Sarren by the shoulders. "What did you do?!"

Sarren's gaze locked onto his. "I didn't open it. The Oathkeepers did."

The Oathkeeper, now barely holding its form together, reached for Sarren. **"You cannot stop what has already begun."**

The monolith erupted.

A force unlike anything they had ever felt surged outward, throwing them across the chamber. Darkness engulfed them. And in the depths of it, something moved.

A whisper, ancient and insidious, echoed through the void.

"Veloria was only the beginning."

Then, silence.

And the world turned upside down.

EPILOGUE

The echoes of Veloria had faded, but the scars remained. Aarav stood at the edge of the research station, gazing at the dark expanse of space beyond the planet. The events of the past days had rewritten everything they thought they knew. Veloria was no longer just a mystery it was a warning, a secret buried beneath layers of time and silence. Sarren watched him quietly, his gaze unreadable. "This is only the beginning," he said, his voice carrying the weight of unseen consequences. Aarav exhaled. He knew that. What they had uncovered, what they had left behind it would not remain buried for long. Earth would have to face the truth. And somewhere, in the depths of space, a new force was already in motion. The fracture had begun.

AFTERWORD

Echoes of Veloria was a journey into the unknown one filled with discovery, danger, and the realization that some secrets are never meant to be unearthed. This book is not just about time loops, extraterrestrial mysteries, and scientific wonders it's about choices, consequences, and the weight of knowledge. The characters have evolved, the stakes have risen, and as we move forward, the story only grows deeper.

The next chapter awaits **The Fractured Oath.**
The universe of LOOPED is far from over.

To everyone who has joined me on this journey, thank you. Your passion and curiosity keep this world alive. Until the next loop stay curious, stay questioning, and never stop looking beyond the stars.

ACKNOWLEDGEMENT

Writing LOOPED has been an incredible journey,

and I want to extend my deepest gratitude to those who played a significant role in making this book a reality.

A special thanks to **Rahul**, for his unwavering support throughout this process. His encouragement and help kept me going when things felt overwhelming.

To **Arjun Vasudev**, who planted the initial idea for LOOPED your spark of imagination set everything in motion.

To **Avi**, my creative assistant, proofreader, writing assistant, and creative partner ; your input, insights, and dedication helped shape this book into what it is today. I couldn't have done this without you. And to everyone who believed in this story your support, enthusiasm, and excitement mean the world to me. LOOPED is just the beginning, and I can't wait to share the rest of the journey with you.

Sathyaraj Natarajan is a Restoration Artist at Prime Focus Technologies, Mumbai, with a deep passion for cinema, technology, and science. Originally from Piravom, Kerala, he brings a unique perspective to his work, blending creativity with technical expertise. His journey into storytelling began with Amma's Love Poetry, his first book of poetry. While his earlier projects, RED WAVE and Breaking Free, remain on hold, they paved the way for his venture into sci-fi fiction, leading to the creation of the LOOPED series. Beyond his work in digital restoration, Sathyaraj is an avid reader and an explorer of the cosmos, fascinated by astronomy and the mysteries of the universe.

BOOKS BY THIS AUTHOR

Amma's Love

This collection of poems is a deeply personal and emotional journey through the life of a young man and his relationship with his mother. The poems explore the joys and sorrows of family, love, and loss, as the author grapples with the challenges of cancer, grief, and the passage of time. From the happy memories of childhood to the heart-wrenching moments of loss and grief, each poem is a powerful and moving exploration of the human experience. The author's vivid imagery and raw emotion bring these poems to life, making them a powerful and moving tribute to the bond between mother and child. With a mix of hope, sorrow, and love, this collection of poems is a must-read for anyone who has ever been touched by the power of family and the human spirit.

LOOPED

LOOPED – A Time-Bending Sci-Fi Thriller

When a team of brilliant scientists stumbles upon an anomaly that defies the laws of time, they
find themselves trapped in an endless cycle of discovery and destruction. As they unravel the
mystery, an enigmatic alien named Sarren emerges with secrets that could alter humanity's fate
forever.

With time slipping through their fingers and an unseen force closing in, Dr. Aarav Menon and
his team must race against the unknown—before they become permanently looped.

A mind-bending journey of time, survival, and cosmic intrigue begins here.

CALL TO ACTION

If you enjoyed **LOOPED** and are eager for more, the journey continues in **Echoes of Veloria** and
beyond! Stay connected for updates on future releases, exclusive content, and behind-the-scenes
insights.
Follow me on social media:
Instagram: ***@thisissamayah***
X (Twitter): ***@thisissamayah***
For inquiries, feedback, or just to share your thoughts, feel free to reach out:
Email: sathyarajn@zohomail.in
Your support means the world, and I can't wait to share whats next in the *LOOPED universe*
with you!

9 789334 254495

Printed at Repro India Ltd.